Daisy the Kitten

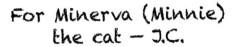

For Minerva (Minnie)
the cat — J.C.

Text Copyright © 2016 by Jane Clarke and Oxford University Press
Illustrations Copyright © 2016 by Oxford University Press

All rights reserved. Published by Scholastic Inc., 557 Broadway,
New York, NY 10012, *Publishers since 1920.* SCHOLASTIC and associated logos
are trademarks and/or registered trademarks of Scholastic Inc. Published
by arrangement with Oxford University Press. Series created
by Oxford University Press.

First published in the United Kingdom in 2015 by Oxford University Press,
Great Clarendon Street, Oxford, OX2 6DP.

The publisher does not have any control over and does not assume any
responsibility for author or third-party websites or their content.

No part of this publication may be reproduced, stored in a retrieval system,
or transmitted in any form or by any means, electronic, mechanical,
photocopying, recording, or otherwise, without written permission
of the publisher. For information regarding permission, write to
Oxford University Press, Rights Department, Great Clarendon Street,
Oxford, OX2 6DP, United Kingdom.

This book is a work of fiction. Names, characters, places, and incidents are
either the product of the author's imagination or are used fictitiously, and any
resemblance to actual persons, living or dead, business establishments,
events, or locales is entirely coincidental.

ISBN 978-0-545-87343-7

10 9 8 7 6 5   18 19 20

Printed in the U.S.A.   23
First printing, August 2016

Book design by Mary Claire Cruz

Daisy the Kitten

Jane Clarke

Scholastic Inc.

Chapter One

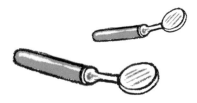

Peanut the mouse wheeled a dentist's chair into the middle of Dr. KittyCat's clinic.

"There's a lot to do on Shiny Smiles day," he squeaked, as he pulled a folding screen around the chair. "And it's the Thistletown Festival, too. Don't forget we're judging the Cupcake Bake-off at three o'clock."

"I can't wait to taste everyone's cupcakes!" Dr. KittyCat meowed. She laid out a row of long, thin, shiny instruments on her desk.

"Dental mirrors, tweezers, probes, scalers . . ." she murmured. "We're ready to go."

Peanut scampered across to the door and opened it. Little animals were waiting in a line outside.

"Come in, everyone," he told them. "Dr. KittyCat's ready to check your shiny smiles." Peanut opened a notebook that said *Furry First-aid Book* on the front cover. It was where Dr. KittyCat kept her medical and dental notes about all the little animals in Thistletown. "Who's first?" he asked.

A small hedgehog stepped forward. His ears were twitching nervously.

"I am," he whispered.

"Follow me . . ." Peanut led him behind the screen.

The hedgehog gave a little squeal when he saw the dentist's chair.

"There's no need to worry,"
Dr. KittyCat meowed. "You're safe
in our paws."

Peanut opened Dr. KittyCat's *Furry
First-aid Book* and flipped through it.
"It's the first time that Bramble has been
to Shiny Smiles," he told Dr. KittyCat
as the young hedgehog scrambled onto
the dentist's chair.

"All you have to do is open your
mouth wide," Peanut instructed, tucking
a bib carefully under Bramble's chin.

Bramble took one look at the row of

shiny dental instruments and clamped his jaws shut. His whiskers began to quiver.

"You need to open your mouth now," Peanut told him gently.

Bramble shook his head and curled up into a prickly ball.

"How can we check Bramble's teeth now?" Peanut squeaked worriedly.

"Don't panic, Peanut," Dr. KittyCat meowed calmly. "It takes some little animals a while to get used to the idea of coming to our Shiny Smiles clinic and having their mouths examined regularly. We don't want to rush things and scare them away." She turned to the little hedgehog.

"It doesn't matter if it takes more than one visit for you to have your teeth checked, Bramble," she reassured him. "It's not an emergency. You don't have to open your mouth if you don't want to."

Bramble slowly uncurled himself and poked his nose out.

Peanut was glad to see that his whiskers had stopped quivering. Bramble smiled a tiny smile that showed a glimpse of his front teeth.

Dr. KittyCat turned to her row of dental instruments and picked up a little mirror on a long, thin handle. She held it up to the nervous hedgehog.

"You have very nice teeth," she purred, "and we want to keep them that way. Next time, do you think you could open your jaws wide enough for me to put this dental mirror in your mouth so I can do a complete check-up?"

I was a purr-fect patient for Dr. KittyCat!

"Yes!" Bramble promised. He scampered down from the chair. "Do I still get a sticker?" he asked anxiously.

"Of course," Dr. KittyCat purred. She handed him a sticker which said: "I was a purr-fect patient for Dr. KittyCat!"

Peanut poked his head around the screen.

"Next!" he called.

A very small and fluffy kitten sprang up onto the dentist's chair and opened her mouth wide, showing all her sharp little baby teeth. Peanut checked his notebook.

"This is Daisy's second visit to our Shiny Smiles clinic, so she knows what to do," he said.

Peanut passed Dr. KittyCat the sterilized mirror and she carefully examined every surface of each one of Daisy's teeth. Then she took a long, thin instrument with a hook on the end and very gently probed between each tooth.

"Daisy, your teeth are purr-fect. You can rinse your mouth out now." Dr. KittyCat smiled. "Your mouth is very healthy. It won't be long before you get your grown-up teeth. One of your teeth has just started to wobble and it will fall out soon," she went on. "Your new teeth will be a lot bigger, especially the long, pointy ones on the sides. They're called canines."

"Your grown-up teeth will look like Dr. KittyCat's," Peanut told her.

"That's good, because when I grow up I want to be just like Dr. KittyCat."

Daisy giggled as she took her sticker and jumped down from the chair.

"Nutmeg!" Daisy called. "It's your turn now. I'll wait for you."

A young guinea pig hopped up onto the dentist's chair.

"My gum is sore," Nutmeg told Dr. KittyCat. "It feels as if something's stuck in it."

"We'll soon sort that out," Dr. KittyCat reassured her. She tucked the bib under Nutmeg's chin and picked out a long, thin pair of tweezers.

"A seed was stuck between your teeth and your gum," Dr. KittyCat

exclaimed, holding it up for Nutmeg
to see. "You must have missed it
when you brushed your teeth.
Peanut will show you how to brush
them properly."

Peanut grabbed a toothbrush. "Don't
just go up and down—go around and
around in tiny circles like this," he
said, as he demonstrated the actions.

"It's important that everyone
brushes their teeth very carefully
every day," Dr. KittyCat
told Nutmeg.

"Especially today," Peanut
said. He handed Nutmeg her
sticker. "Everyone will be eating

sweet things this afternoon at the
Cupcake Bake-off."

"Did you know that anyone who
enters has to make six cupcakes?" Nutmeg
told them excitedly as she jumped
down from the chair. "I'm making seedy
cupcakes with cherries on top."

"Yummy!" Peanut murmured.

"I'm going to make sticky toffee cupcakes with swirly buttercream frosting," Daisy meowed from the other side of the screen.

"Delicious," Dr. KittyCat purred.

"I'm going to use lots of sprinkles," Posy the puppy piped up.

"And I'm putting smiley faces on mine," Fennel the fox cub yipped.

Peanut stuck his head around the screen.

"I can't wait to taste all of your cupcakes!" he squeaked. "Now, let's see—Fennel, are you next?"

By lunchtime, all the little animals'
teeth had been checked. Peanut began
to sterilize the dental instruments
that Dr. KittyCat had used and put
them away.

"Will you need any of these things
before the next Shiny Smiles day?"
he asked.

Dr. KittyCat opened her flowery
doctor's bag and checked the
contents. "Scissors, syringe,
medicines, ointments, instant
cold packs, paw-cleaning
gel, mouth gel, wipes.
Stethoscope, ear thermometer,
tweezers, bandages, gauze,

peppermint candies, reward stickers, my knitting . . . That long, thin dental mirror would be a good thing to add to my bag," she told Peanut. "It's very useful for examining patients' mouths. And I think we should take the surgical head lamp, too."

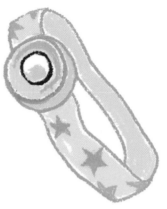

Peanut handed it to her, just as the old-fashioned telephone on the desk began to ring.

Peanut scampered toward the phone—but before he could answer it, Dr. KittyCat stretched out a paw and picked up the handset. She pricked up her furry ears and listened carefully to the call. Peanut's heart began to thump. Who needed their help this time?

Brring!
Brring!

21

"We'll be there in a whisker!"
Dr. KittyCat meowed. She grabbed
her flowery doctor's bag.

"It's Daisy!" Dr. KittyCat told
Peanut. "She's hurt herself at the
Cupcake Bake-off. We're needed there
earlier than we thought!"

Chapter Two

"Poor little Daisy," Peanut squeaked. "I hope she's not badly hurt!" He picked up the *Furry First-aid Book* and hurried after Dr. KittyCat.

The vanbulance was parked in its usual place next to the clinic. Peanut pulled open the flowery door, leaped onto the passenger seat, and tucked in his tail.

Dr. KittyCat threw her flowery doctor's bag onto the front seat next to him and jumped up beside it. She made sure her striped tail was out of the way and closed the door. Peanut glanced over at her as they both clicked in their seatbelts.

"Ready to rescue?" Dr. KittyCat meowed. She grabbed hold of the steering wheel and started the engine.

"Ready to rescue!" Peanut squeaked. He hit the button on the dashboard to make the siren and lights go on.

Nee-nah! Nee-nah! Nee-nah! The vanbulance sped off through Thistletown.

Peanut clutched at the dashboard as the vanbulance bumped and rumbled over Timber Bridge. The tires squealed as they rounded Duckpond Bend and raced along the country lane. Peanut stifled an anxious squeak and tried to keep his whiskers from quivering. *Don't panic, Peanut,* he told himself, *Dr. KittyCat drives fast, but she always drives safely.*

In no time at all they were at
the meadow. With a *scr-ee-eech* of
the brakes, Dr. KittyCat brought the
vanbulance to a halt next to a big,
bright banner that said, "Welcome to
Thistletown Festival!" Peanut sighed
with relief as he turned off the lights
and siren and jumped out.

The festival field was crammed full
of brightly colored tents.

Peanut read the signs. "Storytelling, clay-pot making, music, dancing, knitting . . . Something different's going on in every tent," he squeaked. "Where's the Cupcake Bake-off taking place?"

Dr. KittyCat pointed to a large canvas tent at the far end of the field. Two flags, each with a picture of a cupcake, and a string of colorful bunting fluttered in the breeze above the tent.

"In that tent," Dr. KittyCat said, leading the way toward it. "So that's where Daisy must be . . ."

Mrs. Hazelnut greeted them at the entrance. "Thank goodness you're here," she said.

Inside the tent, a group of little
animals wearing aprons and chefs' hats
was gathered around what looked like
a small and very fluffy ball of fur. It was
Daisy. The tiny kitten was curled up
on the wooden floor beside one of the
baking stations. She was crying as if her
heart would break.

Dr. KittyCat and Peanut made
a beeline toward her. Dr. KittyCat set
down her flowery doctor's bag next
to the fluffy kitten.

"We're here now, Daisy," she
purred. "Tell us what's wrong."

Daisy's nose was covered in flour and tears were rolling down her fluffy cheeks. She waved a paw at the flour-speckled counter. Seven tiny cupcakes were sitting on a cooling rack in the middle of a sticky jumble of mixing bowls, spoons, and baking pans.

"I need to put frosting on my cupcakes," Daisy wailed. "But I can't do it. It hurts too much!"

"We'll make you better as soon as we find out what the problem is," Dr. KittyCat reassured her.

Dr. KittyCat smiled up at Mrs. Hazelnut and the little animals. "Daisy is safe in our paws," she told them. "Please get on with making your cupcakes while we help her."

Peanut turned to Daisy. "Now, Daisy," he squeaked. "You told us about your cupcakes, but what Dr. KittyCat really needs to know is exactly what part of you is hurting . . ."

Chapter
Three

The tiny kitten looked up at Peanut
and Dr. KittyCat and blinked her
tear-filled eyes.

"It's my mouth," she sobbed.
"It's very sore."

"Your mouth?" Peanut squeaked.
"Your mouth was fine a couple of
hours ago at our Shiny Smiles clinic.

Dr. KittyCat even said how healthy it was."

A picture of Dr. KittyCat holding a long, thin dental probe with a sharp hook on the end popped into Peanut's mind. Had Dr. KittyCat accidentally nicked Daisy's mouth with one of her dental instruments and made it sore?

Peanut gave a little *Eek!*

Dr. KittyCat looked at him curiously. "Is anything the matter, Peanut?" she asked. "You're not panicking, are you?"

"No, nothing's the matter," Peanut squeaked. He took a deep breath. *Of course Dr. KittyCat hasn't hurt Daisy,* he

told himself. *She's very well trained, and she's always so careful and gentle.*

Dr. KittyCat opened her flowery doctor's bag and took out the little mirror on the long, thin handle.

"I want you to open your mouth wide," she told Daisy, "like you did at the Shiny Smiles clinic this morning."

"I can't." Daisy snuffled. "It hurts too much," she mumbled between clenched teeth. "I heard you tell Bramble he didn't have to open his mouth unless he wanted to. Well, I wanted to this morning, but I don't want to now!"

"But I can only find out what's

wrong and make it better if you let me look inside your mouth," Dr. KittyCat explained. "I promise I'll be very careful not to hurt you. Do you think you could try to open it a little?"

Daisy blinked her tear-filled eyes and reluctantly nodded her head.

"You are a brave kitten," Dr. KittyCat purred as Daisy slowly opened her mouth.

"What can you see?" Peanut asked anxiously.

"I can't see very much at all," Dr. KittyCat meowed. "I need a little more light."

Peanut reached into Dr. KittyCat's

bag and took out her
surgical head lamp.
He helped her adjust
it and watched as Dr. KittyCat very
carefully examined the inside of Daisy's
mouth with her dental mirror.

"I can't see anything seriously
wrong, and there's no swelling,"
Dr. KittyCat reassured the little kitten.
"But your tongue and gums are very
pink." She took off the head lamp and
handed it to Peanut to put away.

"My mouth is so sore!"
Daisy meowed.

Peanut flicked through
Dr. KittyCat's *Furry First-aid Book*.

"Does Daisy have anything stuck between her teeth and gums, like the seed you removed from Nutmeg's mouth this morning?" he asked.

"I checked and I couldn't see anything like that," Dr. KittyCat told him. "Daisy's teeth aren't as clean as they were. In fact, they're covered in cake crumbs, but cake wouldn't make her mouth sore . . ."

"Does she have any other symptoms?" Peanut asked.

Dr. KittyCat looked Daisy over carefully.

"Her eyes are clear and bright, her ears are pricked, and her fur is smooth

and glossy," Dr. KittyCat murmured.
"She doesn't look sick at all."

"Do you have a sore throat, Daisy?"
she asked.

Daisy shook her head.

"Or a headache, or a sore tummy?"
Again, Daisy shook her head.

"Does anywhere else hurt at all,
even a little bit?" Dr. KittyCat asked.

Daisy paused before she spoke.
"My paws were sore a little while ago,"
she meowed, "but they feel better now."
She held out her front paws for
Dr. KittyCat to see.

"Hmm," Dr. KittyCat murmured.
"Your paw pads are a little pink."

"Eek!" Peanut squeaked in alarm. "It's not pawpox, is it?" There had recently been an outbreak of pawpox in Thistletown, but there hadn't been any new cases for a while.

"It can't be pawpox," Dr. KittyCat said calmly. "Daisy's already had that, remember?"

"Of course, you can't get it more than once." Peanut sighed with relief.

"There is a rare illness called paw and mouth that causes pinkness in mouth and paws," Dr. KittyCat said thoughtfully.

Peanut stifled another *Eek! I shouldn't worry the patient*, he told himself.

"Paw and mouth is a very mild illness," Dr. KittyCat said reassuringly. "So mild it is often missed. It causes a rise in the patient's body temperature along with the pink mouth and paws. I'll check to see if Daisy has a fever . . ."

Peanut took the ear thermometer out of Dr. KittyCat's bag and put on a fresh hygiene cover before handling it to her.

"I'm just going to put this in your ear and hold it there until it beeps," she told Daisy.

Beep! Beep! Beep!

Dr. KittyCat examined the reading on the thermometer.

"Daisy's temperature is absolutely normal for a kitten," Dr. KittyCat declared. "So she doesn't have paw and mouth."

Then what is wrong with Daisy? Peanut wondered. He gazed around the tent at the little animals busily making and decorating their cupcakes. *Most of them are making eight cupcakes even though the competition is for six,* he thought. *That must be in case one or two*

*of the cupcakes go wrong and they have to
throw them away* . . .

"Oh!" Peanut squeaked. "I think
I know what's wrong with Daisy!"

Chapter Four

"How many cupcakes did you bake?"
Peanut gently asked Daisy.

"Eight." Daisy snuffled. "All of them
were purr-fect!"

"Did you wear oven mitts when
you took them out of the oven?" Peanut
went on.

"Yes!" Daisy meowed. "That was

one of the rules. There are lots of rules."

Peanut nodded thoughtfully. He looked at the floor. There was a little heap of crumbs in one spot.

"Did one of your cakes fall on the floor?" Peanut squeaked.

Daisy nodded.

"Did you take off the oven mitts to pick it up?" Peanut went on.

"Yes." Daisy sniffed.

Peanut turned to Dr. KittyCat. "That explains why Daisy's paw pads are pink," he murmured. Dr. KittyCat nodded.

"Daisy, was that eighth cupcake still very hot when you tasted it?" Peanut asked the tiny kitten.

"Yes!" Daisy squeaked. "I blew on it, but the toffee pieces inside were still really hot," she whispered.

"That explains everything," Peanut said. "You burned your paws and mouth by handling and eating a cupcake

while it was too hot. Why didn't you
tell us that right away?"

Daisy hung her head. "Because we
weren't supposed to eat any cupcakes
that fell on the floor," she wailed. "We
were supposed to throw them away.
I didn't want to get into trouble!"

"Mrs. Hazelnut's much too busy to be upset with you," Peanut squeaked comfortingly.

Dr. KittyCat smiled. "You worked everything out like a detective, Peanut. I'm very proud of you."

I'm proud of me, too, thought Peanut.

"Now that we know what's wrong, we can treat you, Daisy," Dr. KittyCat meowed.

"Your burns aren't serious. You should really have run your paws under cold water the instant you felt the burn, but never mind. Your paws are already getting better on their own, and the skin isn't broken, so they don't need any treatment . . ."

"But what about my mouth?" Daisy cried. "It still hurts!"

"I can make that feel better right away." Dr. KittyCat opened her flowery doctor's bag and took out a small tube. "Here's some nice soothing gel that will work very quickly."

Dr. KittyCat squeezed a little mound of wobbly gel onto Daisy's paw and told her to rub it gently over her tongue and gums.

"Mmm," Daisy murmured. "That feels nice and cool. And it tastes all minty fresh, like toothpaste."

She gave a little purr. "I feel much better now. I can continue making the buttercream frosting to decorate my cupcakes!"

Daisy poured powdered sugar into a bowl and added a big lump of butter.

"You might need to rub more gel onto your tongue and gums in an hour or so," Dr. KittyCat advised. She put the cap back on the tube of gel and handed it to Daisy.

"Thank you!" Daisy popped the gel into her apron pocket. Peanut couldn't

help smiling as the kitten held an
enormous wooden spoon between
her tiny paws and began to mix her
frosting. A cloud of powdered sugar
flew into the air.

Ak . . . aak! Daisy spluttered.

There was a surprised *Yip!* from
the counter next to hers. Peanut looked
just in time to see Fennel almost drop
a tray of steaming cupcakes as he lifted
them from the oven.

"You made me jump, Daisy!" the
fox cub grumbled as he turned his

cupcakes onto a cooling rack and took
off his oven mitts.

"Sorry, Fennel," Daisy meowed.
"Some sugar got up my nose. I'm really
glad you didn't burn yourself. Burns
hurt a lot!"

"That was almost a bad accident,"
Peanut whispered to Dr. KittyCat.

"And there's another accident waiting to happen . . ." Dr. KittyCat pointed to another baking station. Peanut followed her gaze. Posy the puppy was splattered from head to tail with cake mix—and she had her nose almost pressed to the glass door of her oven.

Peanut hurried up to the
sticky puppy.

"Posy, be careful! You'll burn
your nose," he squeaked anxiously.
"Your cupcakes will bake without you
watching them!"

Posy took a step back and wagged
her tail sheepishly. A glob of cake mix
flew off her tail and hit Peanut on the
ear.

Splat!

Mrs. Hazelnut rushed over,
looking worried.

"Mrs. Hazelnut," Dr. KittyCat
meowed. "I think Peanut and I should
stay to keep an eye on Daisy, and just in

case there are any other mishaps with cupcakes."

"Thank you!" Mrs. Hazelnut exclaimed. "It will be a while before all the cupcakes are finished for the judging session and I'm finding it hard to watch over everyone."

"We'll be ready to rescue if you need us!" Peanut reassured her.

Chapter Five

"This is the judging table." Mrs. Hazelnut led Peanut and Dr. KittyCat to a round table covered in a checkered tablecloth. "Make yourselves comfortable," she said, pulling out two chairs.

Peanut put Dr. KittyCat's *Furry First-aid Book* down on the table and began to write up his notes on Daisy.

Dr. KittyCat rummaged in her flowery doctor's bag and took out her knitting.

"This little hat I'm knitting will look really cute on you, Peanut," she purred. "I'll leave little holes for your ears . . ."

"Er . . . um . . . thanks, Dr. KittyCat," Peanut mumbled. He didn't like knitted hats, but how could he tell Dr. KittyCat without hurting her feelings? He glanced up at the scene in the tent. The little animals had

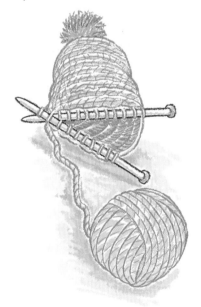

finished making their cupcakes and were busily cleaning up the mess with sponges, tea towels, and mops.

"Time to judge the cupcakes!" Mrs. Hazelnut declared at last. "Daisy, you're up first."

Daisy proudly carried her cake stand of cupcakes to the table and set it down in front of Peanut and Dr. KittyCat.

"I've made sticky toffee cupcakes with buttercream swirl," she declared.

Peanut smiled. There was so much buttercream on the top of Daisy's cupcakes that they looked like upside-down ice cream cones. And the little

kitten looked as if she'd been dusted
from head to tail with frosting.

Peanut picked up a cupcake and
took a nibble. A big piece of toffee
came away in his mouth.

"Mrrm," he mumbled. "My teeth
are stuck together!"

Dr. KittyCat took a lick of
buttercream.

"Delicious!" she exclaimed.

"Nutmeg next," Mrs. Hazelnut
announced. "Nutmeg's made seedy
cupcakes with cherries on top."

Peanut sucked the toffee off his

teeth and took a big bite out of one of the guinea pig's cupcakes.

"That's my kind of cupcake," he squeaked. "Yum!"

"They're a little dry for me," Dr. KittyCat said thoughtfully. She picked out a piece of seed from between her teeth. "But they've given me an idea. If I put a little red pom-pom on the hat I'm knitting, you will look just like one of Nutmeg's cherry cupcakes when you're wearing it!"

Peanut shuddered. "I think you should give the hat to Nutmeg," he suggested hurriedly. "I wouldn't mind at all."

"That's a great idea," Dr. KittyCat
meowed.

Peanut breathed a sigh of relief as the
next contestant came up to the table.

"I've put lots of sprinkles on my
cupcakes," Posy woofed.

"I can see that." Peanut looked at the sticky puppy and chuckled. "There are lots of sprinkles stuck to your fur, too."

"Posy's cupcakes look a little messy," Dr. KittyCat commented. "But they are nice and light and moist."

"The flavor's very good, too," mumbled Peanut, with his mouth full of crumbs.

"Don't eat too much of each cupcake," Dr. KittyCat warned him. "There are still cupcakes from five other young bakers to go . . ."

At last, Peanut and Dr. KittyCat had tasted all the cupcakes. Cupcakes with buttercream, cupcakes with sprinkles, cupcakes with smiley faces, seedy cupcakes, crunchy nut cupcakes, butterfly cupcakes with fondant frosting, honeycomb cupcakes, and, finally, Willow the duckling's white chocolate cupcakes. Peanut wasn't sure he wanted to see another cupcake ever again.

"Who do you think should be the winner?" Dr. KittyCat asked Peanut.

"It's too hard to choose," Peanut said. "Some looked a lot better than they tasted and others tasted a lot better than they looked. I liked the taste of the seedy and nutty ones best."

"And I liked the ones with buttercream." Dr. KittyCat laughed. "I think the fairest thing is to call it a tie."

"That's a great idea," Peanut squeaked.

Dr. KittyCat stood up. "You have all made wonderful cupcakes," she declared. "Peanut and I have found it very, very hard to choose the winner. But after a lot of discussion, we have made our decision. The winner is . . ."

She paused. Silence
fell inside the tent.
Peanut smiled—all the
little animals looked as if
they were holding their breath . . .

"EVERYONE!"

"Woo-hoo!" All the little animals
jumped up and down and cheered as
Peanut handed out "Cupcake Bake-off
Winner" badges to everyone.

"And now," Dr. KittyCat
announced, "it's time to eat the
cupcakes!"

The tent filled with the sound of
little animals nibbling and chomping.

Cupcake
Bake-off
Winner

"Time to go!" Peanut squeaked. Dr. KittyCat picked up her bag and put it on the table.

"I'll be ready in a whisker. I just need to put my knitting away . . ." she meowed.

Daisy hurried up to them. She handed Dr. KittyCat a small package wrapped in paper.

"I saved you both a cupcake to thank you very much for making me feel better today," she told them.

"Thank you, Daisy," Dr. KittyCat purred. "We'll save them for later, won't we, Peanut?"

Peanut nodded.

"My tummy is really
full right now,"
he squeaked.

Dr. KittyCat
opened her bag
and put her knitting and Daisy's
present inside.

"You were so busy decorating your
cupcakes, I forgot to give you a sticker,"
she told Daisy. "Would you like one?"

"Yes, please!" Daisy's eyes lit up as
Dr. KittyCat handed her a sticker
which said: "I was a purr-fect patient
for Dr. KittyCat!"

"Uh-oh," Peanut squeaked. "I think
we have another patient."

I was a
purr-fect
patient for
Dr. KittyCat!

Fennel was making his way to their
table with his tail between his legs.
"Dr. KittyCat," he groaned, "I've eaten
too many cupcakes and I feel sick."

"I have just the thing for that."
Dr. KittyCat opened her bag and
took out a little box.

"Suck on this peppermint candy," she told Fennel. "It will settle your tummy in no time at all."

"Thank you," Fennel yipped.

"May I please have a sticker like Daisy's?"

"Of course!" Dr. KittyCat said, and she handed him one.

Soon there was a line of little animals all asking for peppermint candies and stickers. There were just enough to go around.

"It was hard to tell who had eaten too many cupcakes and who just wanted a sticker," Dr. KittyCat meowed as they made their way back to the vanbulance.

"Everyone wanted one of your stickers." Peanut smiled. "But I think they'd all eaten too many cupcakes, as well."

"You ate a lot of cupcakes, too," Dr. KittyCat said. "How are you feeling?"

"Fine!" Peanut squeaked as he jumped into the vanbulance. "How about you?"

Dr. KittyCat said nothing, but smiled at Peanut uncertainly.

Chapter Six

The vanbulance chugged down the
narrow lane through Thistletown.

"You're driving much more slowly
than usual," Peanut commented.

"There's no hurry on the way back,"
Dr. KittyCat meowed. "It's good to take
it easy."

She pressed one paw to her mouth. Her whiskers twitched.

"Are you feeling OK?" Peanut asked as Dr. KittyCat carefully steered the vanbulance around Duckpond Bend.

Dr. KittyCat cleared her throat.

"My tummy does feel a little sick,"
she confessed. "But maybe it's just the
bumps in the road and nothing to do
with the cupcakes."

Peanut wasn't sure he believed her.
He didn't want to admit it, but he was
beginning to feel a little bit sick himself.
He swallowed hard as the vanbulance
bumped slowly over Timber Bridge and
rumbled to a halt outside Dr. KittyCat's
clinic.

It was time to pack up the Shiny Smiles
equipment. Peanut slowly folded away
the screen and wheeled the dentist's
chair into the corner.

"It's been another busy day,"
Peanut squeaked. "We saw an awful lot
of patients."

"And an awful lot of cupcakes,"
Dr. KittyCat meowed, as she bent down
and opened her bag. She swished her
striped tail.

"More cupcakes," she groaned,
holding up Daisy's present. "Do you
want one, Peanut?"

"I'll save it for tomorrow," Peanut
told Dr. KittyCat. "Right now, I would
like one of your peppermint
candies instead!"

"That's a very good idea,"
Dr. KittyCat meowed. "There's a new
box in the supplies closet. I think I'll
have one, too."

Peanut and Dr. KittyCat sat down

in their chairs and sucked on their
peppermints.

"That's better." Peanut sighed.

Dr. KittyCat took her knitting out
of her bag.

"You did really well today,"
Dr. KittyCat told Peanut, as she clicked
away with her knitting needles. "For a
while I was puzzled about what was
wrong with Daisy."

"I was puzzled, too," Peanut
admitted, "until I counted her cupcakes."

"I'd hate to count how many
cupcakes we tasted today,"
Dr. KittyCat murmured.

"At least eight each," Peanut told her.

"That's far too much sugar for one day," Dr. KittyCat declared. "It's the main cause of dental decay."

"Eek!" Peanut squeaked. "I don't want my teeth to fall out!"

"Don't panic, Peanut," Dr. KittyCat told him. "Your teeth won't fall out if you clean them carefully."

Peanut jumped to his feet. "I'm going to brush my teeth NOW," he squeaked.

Dr. KittyCat put down her knitting. "So am I," she meowed. "And that way, we'll both keep our shiny smiles!"

The end

What's in Dr. KittyCat's bag?

Here are just some of the things that Dr. KittyCat always carries in her flowery doctor's bag.

Dental mirror

Dr. KittyCat uses her dental mirror to examine her patients' teeth and gums. She finds its long, thin handle very useful, as it helps her to see right to the back of her patients' mouths.

Cooling gel

When her patients have sore mouths, Dr. KittyCat tells them to gently rub a little bit of cooling gel over the area where it hurts. The gel stops the swelling and soothes the pain. It also contains antiseptic, which stops infection and speeds up the healing process.

Bandages

Bandages are used for covering up cuts and scrapes, to protect the wound and make sure that dirt doesn't get inside. They come in all kinds of patterns, including stars and butterflies, but Peanut's favorites are the ones covered in little paw prints.

Peppermint candies

Peppermint candies are excellent for settling upset tummies. Dr. KittyCat always carries some in her bag for those times when she gets that "too full" feeling, because she knows that peppermint relaxes the muscles in the tummy.

Dr. KittyCat is ready to rescue:
Posy the Puppy

"I'll go in and keep her calm while
we both figure out the best way to treat
her and get her out," Peanut suggested.

"Good idea," said Dr. KittyCat.
"Take a cold pack with you." She
opened her flowery doctor's bag.

"Oooh!" The curious crowd pushed
forward to get a better look.

Peanut scurried into the tunnel.

There was just enough sunlight shining through the tough canvas for him to make out a bundle of quivering golden fur. The fluffy little puppy was curled up in a tight ball in the gloom.

"I'm here now, Posy," he murmured.

A rubbery nose poked out of the fur ball. "Ow!" she yelped.

Don't panic, Peanut!

A note from the author:

Jane says . . .

"Our kitten, Minnie, liked to lie on her back on the floor and claw her way under the sofa and out the other side. One day she didn't come out. She'd shredded the material so badly she'd got caught up in it and needed to be cut out!"

See you next time!

Visit Friendship Forest, where animals can talk and magic exists!

Meet best friends Jess and Lily and their adorable animal pals in this enchanting new series from the creator of Rainbow Magic!

SCHOLASTIC

scholastic.com

MAGICAF